RONY'S VILLAGE ADVENTURES

TEJASWI DALVI

Made with ♥ on the Notion Press Platform
www.notionpress.com

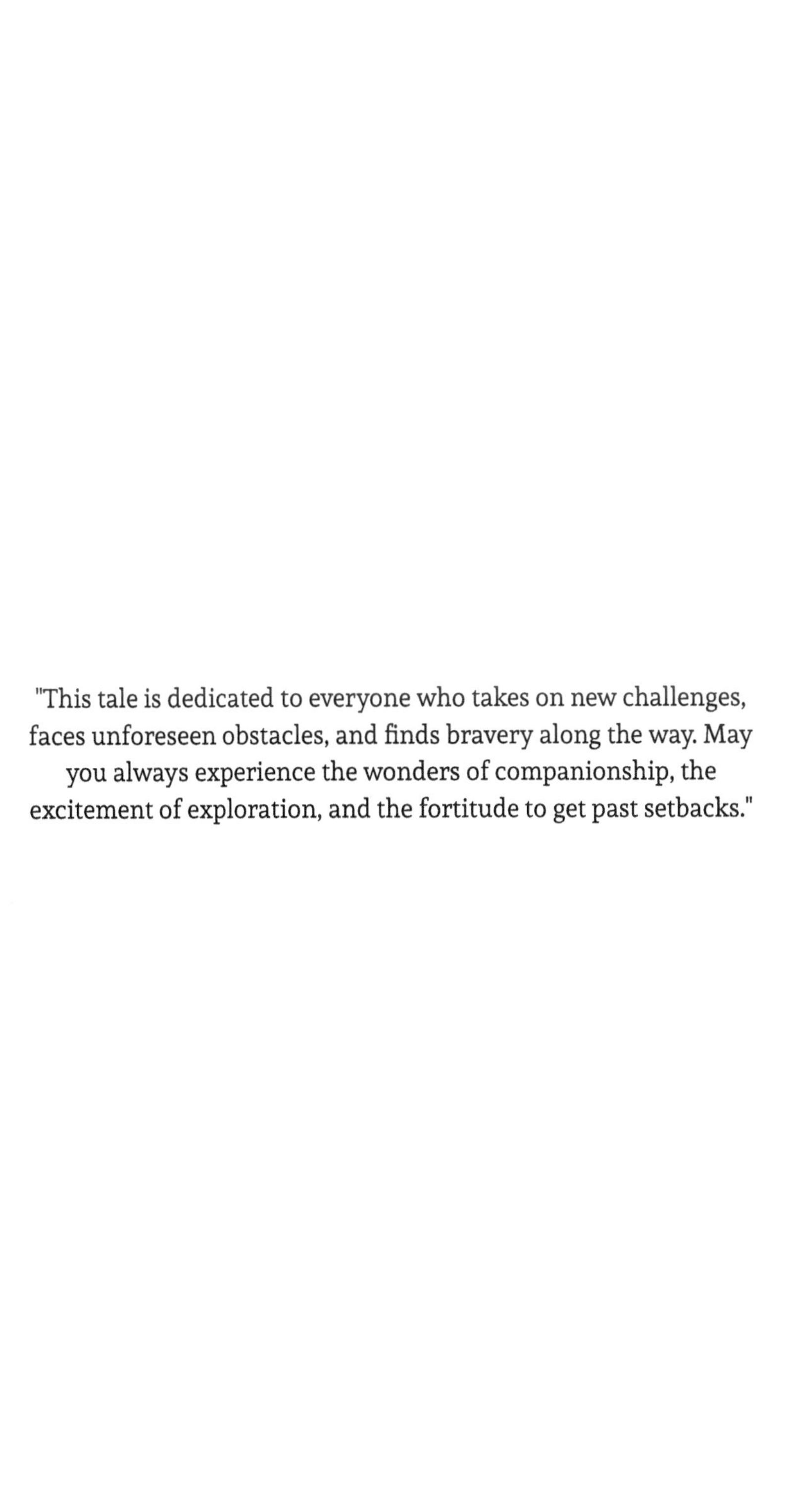

"This tale is dedicated to everyone who takes on new challenges, faces unforeseen obstacles, and finds bravery along the way. May you always experience the wonders of companionship, the excitement of exploration, and the fortitude to get past setbacks."

Contents

Foreword

Introduction:

Readers will travel on an engrossing trip with Rony, a young protagonist in "City to Village Adventures," as he makes the transition from the busy mysteries of the city to the peaceful ones of rural life. This story encourages readers of all ages to investigate the ties of friendship, the excitement of adventure, and the resiliency of the human spirit through turns and turns, unexpected discoveries, and bravery-filled moments. I hope that when you read the pages of this narrative, the experiences ahead will bring you joy, inspiration, and a fresh sense of wonder.

Acknowledgements

My sincere appreciation goes out to everyone who helped make "Rony's Village Adventures" possible.

Thank you to my family, friends, and loved ones for your continuous encouragement, support, and faith in my storytelling endeavours. You have always been an inspiration to me because of your presence in my life.

I want to thank all of my readers for joining Rony and his companions on this exciting journey. Your curiosity and excitement inspire me to make stories, and it is a pleasure to accompany you on this adventure.

I am incredibly appreciative of the editors, beta readers, and reviewers who helped me with the writing process by offering insightful criticism and direction. Your observations have greatly influenced the final form of this narrative.

Furthermore, I wish to extend my sincere appreciation to Mr. Shrinivas Sharangpani, a distinguished writer and author, for his unwavering encouragement throughout the process of writing this book, as well as his invaluable assistance in reviewing its content.

1

Grown up as tech-savvy teenager

Ranveer was a 12-year-old boy popularly known as Rony who lived in the bustling city of Pune. He was always fascinated by technology and had an unstable curiosity to learn more about it.

Ranveer was always eager to get his hands on different types of gadgets and find out how they worked.

Despite his young age, Ranveer was incredibly knowledgeable about technology. He spent most of his free time reading tech blogs, watching YouTube videos, and tinkering with electronics. He had even built his computer from scratch and programmed a few simple games.

Ranveer's parents were proud of his passion for technology and encouraged him to follow his interests. They often took him to tech events and expos in the city.

Ranveer was the intelligent student in his school for any tech-related questions or issues. His classmates admired his knowledge and would often ask him for help with their projects.

Enter Caption

Ranveer was not only brilliant in technology but also a well-rounded individual. He enjoyed playing different games, reading books of science fiction, adventures, and mysteries, and spending time with his friends and family. His parents made sure that he maintained a balance between his passion for technology and his other interests.

He was a brilliant and curious young boy with a bright future ahead of him. His love for technology would undoubtedly take him on a path of discovery and innovation, and his passion would inspire others to chase their dreams.

Rony was a tech-savvy teenager who was always carrying the latest gadgets with him. He had a smartwatch with all sorts of apps and a pair of high-tech binoculars that he used to spy on wildlife.

Rony's parents and grandparents were very supportive of his love for technology and were always looking for ways to encourage him. On his 12th birthday, they surprised him with two amazing gifts that he had been dreaming of for months.

His parents gifted him a high-tech drone with a high-resolution camera and advanced features like GPS tracking and obstacle avoidance. Ranveer was so grateful for this gift and spent hours exploring the capabilities of the drone. He quickly became an expert at flying it and even started using it to capture stunning aerial footage of his neighborhood and local landmarks.

His friends also enjoyed spending time with Rony and his drone. Ranveer's grandparents, who always cared about his interests, gifted him a brand-new bicycle with the latest technology. The bicycle was equipped with a digital display that showed the speed, distance traveled, and other useful information. It also had an electric motor that allowed Ranveer to pedal with less effort and cover longer distances without getting tired. With his new drone and bicycle, Rony had two amazing tools to arouse his passion for technology and adventure.

When it comes to looks, Rony was a handsome and humble young boy who was the favorite of his friend circle. Rony's signature look was a combination of half-jeans pants and a t-shirt that added a pop of personality to his outfit. Rony loved to wear a white pair of shoes that gave him a stylish look. To complete his look, Rony always wore a cap with the letter "R" printed on it which made him look even more confident.

Although Rony was an introverted person, he was a loyal friend and would go out of his way to help those in need. He had a small circle of close friends whom he trusted. His parents were busy in their professional lives, and Rony often found solace in his books and Gadgets.

He preferred city life and enjoyed spending time outdoors. He loved going for walks in the park, bird-watching, and exploring the hidden nooks and crannies of the city. He observed things very carefully and often noticed them that others missed. This made him an excellent detective in his own right.

Rony's family was a close-knit one, even though both his parents were busy professionals. His father was a bank manager in Pune city, and his mother was a doctor at a 'lifeline' hospital near their house. They both worked long hours, but they always made time for Rony and his younger sister Ruhi.

Rony's father was a tall and imposing man with a stern demeanor. He was well-respected in the community for his integrity and hard work. He had a systematic attitude towards his work and expected the same attitude from his children.

Rony's mother was warm and nurturing. She had a kind heart and a gentle touch,

which made her a favorite among her patients. She was always there to listen to her children's problems and offer comfort to them. Rony's younger sister, Ruhi, was the complete opposite of him. She was outgoing and sociable, and she loved spending time with her friends. Though both siblings were different totally, Rony and Ruhi were close and would often confide in each other about their hopes and fears.

In general, Rony's family was a loving and supportive one. His parent's dedication to their work and their children, along with their shared love for exploring the city, helped shape Rony into the person he was. As Rony was born and brought up in the city he loved the hustle and bustle of life there. He was always eager to explore new places and try new things. The city was full of endless opportunities for adventure and excitement for him.

Exploring many parks and outdoor spaces in the city was Rony's favorite thing to do on weekends. He loved to ride his new bicycle along the city's scenic trails, play football at the local ground, and sometimes go for long walks in the city's many green spaces. He was always amazed by the beauty of the city's parks and the many different activities they offered.

Rony also enjoyed exploring the city's many museums and cultural landmarks. He loved to learn about the city's history and culture and was always amazed by the stories and artifacts on display. He would spend hours wandering through the exhibits and soaking up all the information he could. In addition to his love of outdoor spaces and cultural landmarks, Rony also enjoyed the thrill of city life. Rony's love for the city was rooted in his curiosity and sense of adventure. The Pune city was a place where he could explore, learn, and grow, and he was always excited to see what the next day would bring.

2

Reluctant Relocation

One day Rony was preparing to go to school when his father announced his transfer order to the village that they hadn't visited and which was very far from Pune. It was at the boundary of Maharashtra state of India. They had to move from Pune in the next month. The news of moving from Pune came as a shock to Rony, and it left him feeling uncertain and anxious about the future. As a city boy, he had grown up with the fast-paced and exciting lifestyle of city life, and the prospect of moving to a village seemed daunting and unfamiliar.

Rony's mind was flooded with questions and concerns. He wondered what life in the village would be like, whether he would make new friends, and how he would adjust to a completely different way of life with no basic amenities. He was worried about leaving behind the familiarity and comfort of his city life and starting anew in a completely different environment.

Rony felt like he was being uprooted from everything he loved, and he could not decline in this matter. He was angry with his father for taking away his friendly surroundings and forcing him to start over in an unfamiliar place. Rony's emotions were running high, and he struggled to come to terms with the news. He spent days feeling sad and angry, and he refused to talk about the move with his parents or anyone else.

His parents sensed his distress and tried to reassure him. They explained the reasons behind the move.

They told him about the new opportunities and experiences that awaited them in the village, and how the move would benefit the family in the long run.

However, with time and patience, Rony eventually began to accept the idea of the move. He realized that he couldn't change the situation and that he needed to make the best of it. He slowly started to warm up to the idea of living in a small village and the adventure that awaited him there.

He got curious and excited about the new opportunities in the village and was eager to experience the different cultures. He was delighted about the prospect of making new friends, discovering new places, and learning about the unique customs and traditions of the village.

Rony's situation of mind was one of mixed emotions. On the one hand, he was anxious and uncertain about the future, and on the other hand, he was curious and thrilled about the new opportunities that lay ahead. He knew that he would need time to adjust to the new environment, but he was ready to face the challenge with an open mind and a positive attitude.

As the time for the move to the village drew near, Rony's parents started to prepare for the transition. Rony went to visit his friends one last time.

His friends were also in a similar situation. All the friends also got emotional thinking that such a good friend would not meet again soon and would miss the fun that they all shared. Promised them to meet again, Rony returned home with a heavy heart.

Rony and his family had been busy packing up their belongings and getting ready for the move. They had sorted through their belongings, deciding what to keep and what to give away or sell. Rony had gone through his room. He carefully packed up his books, toys, his favorite gadgets, and electronics including smartwatches, his drone, tablet, and other belongings that he wanted to take with him to the village.

He made sure that he had enough batteries and storage space to keep his devices running smoothly. He was very cautious about everything he needed to stay connected and entertained in the new environment. He also kept the photo frame carefully in his bag which his friends gifted him.

As the day of the move approached, Rony's nerves began to build. He knew that he would miss his friends and the familiar surroundings of the city. He spent time talking with his family, discussing their plans for the move, and sharing his feelings and concerns.

With his nervousness, Rony was determined to approach the move with a positive attitude. He knew that there would be challenges and difficulties ahead, but he was also excited about the opportunity to learn and grow in the new environment. He was ready to embrace the adventure and start a new chapter of his life in the village. The journey started.

3

New Beginnings in an Unfamiliar Place

The journey to the village was long, and Rony spent most of his time in city memories. He looked out the car window and watched as the cityscape slowly gave way to open fields and farmland.

The streets became narrower, and the buildings grew smaller and more spread out. After traveling for more than 8 hours they finally reached their destination.

As they entered the village, Rony felt like he had stepped back in time. The streets were quiet and unpaved, and the houses were of mud and brick. He noticed that there were no tall buildings, no neon lights, and no bustling crowds. Rony felt out of place and unsure of how to act in this new environment. He worried that he wouldn't fit in and that the people in the village would judge him for being a city boy.

As the days passed, He was prepared to make the best of the situation and learn as much as possible about the village and its people. He looked forward to exploring the countryside, meeting new people, and experiencing a different way of life.

As Rony spent more time in the village, he began to understand the rhythm and pace of life there. He learned that life in the village was much slower and more relaxed than in the city and that people took time to appreciate and enjoy the simple pleasures of life. He observed that people in the village had a friendly community where everyone knew each other and looked out for one another. He noticed that people were welcoming and that they enjoyed gathering together for festivals, fairs, and other celebrations.

Rony also learned that life in the village was very different from life in the city in terms of daily routines and chores. He discovered that people in the village started their day early to tend to their farms and animals and that they had a strong connection to the land and nature.

As Rony explored the countryside, he started to appreciate the beauty and simplicity of rural life. He enjoyed the fresh air, green fields, and the quietness that surrounded him. He also learned about the importance of agriculture and farming, and how it was the backbone of the village economy.

Rony came to realize that life in the village was not without its challenges. He saw that people in the village faced difficulties with access to basic things like healthcare and education and realized that there were a small number of job opportunities compared to the city.

With these challenges, Rony grew to appreciate the slower pace of life in the village, and he began to value the importance of community and connectedness that he found there. He learned that life was not just about material possessions and superficial pleasures, but it was about the simple joys of everyday living and the people around us.

4

First Day in the Village School

On the first day of school in the village, Rony was greeted by a group of boys who seemed less friendly.

"Hey, look who it is. The new kid."

Another one replied to him,

"Yeah, I heard he's from the city. I think he's better than us."

Rony was calm. But both the boys were giving him a strange look.

"Um, hi. I'm Rony. Nice to meet you."

The boys were angry with Rony. They felt a little insecure by Rony's presence.

"We don't need to know your name. You're just another city boy trying to show off here. Some children are pleased by you, but we are not."

The other one talked rudely "Yeah, you're not welcome here. Go back to where you came from."

Rony tried to make them understand what his situation was.

"I'm not trying to show off. I just moved here with my family. I want to make friends and learn about the village."

But these boys were not ready to accept Rony as their classmate.

"We don't need any city boys to teach us anything. We know everything we need to know. And it is sufficient for us."

"Yeah, and we don't like outsiders coming in and trying to change things."

Rony was confused by their behaviour and explained.

"I'm not trying to change anything. I just want to be part of the community and make new friends as I am a newcomer. Nothing else."

Rony initiated his hand to shake with the boys.

But the boy shook Rony's hand and warned him "Well, you're not making any friends here.

You're just a city boy and you always will be."

Both the boys left there.

Rony felt hurt and confused by the boy's hostility. He didn't understand why they were so angry and unwelcoming. He felt like an outsider and wished he could go back to the city where he felt more accepted.

During the break between classes, a group of boys approached Rony and started making fun of him. They mocked his city accent, his clothes, and his hobbies. They call him names like "*city slicker*" and "*fancy pants.*"

Rony felt embarrassed and ashamed, and he didn't know how to react in this situation. He had never experienced this kind of bullying before and didn't know how to respond. He wanted to run away and hide. He ran from school to home in between recess. Rony's father was surprised and concerned when he saw his son crying. He sat down with Rony and asked.

"Rony, what's wrong? Why are you crying?"

Rony was talking with frustration.

"Daddy, I don't want to go back to school. The boys there were mean to me."

"What boys? What happened?"
Rony's father was surprised by his answer.

"They bullied me. They called me a city boy and said I didn't belong there. They were mean."

Father felt bad about the boy's behaviour.

"I'm so sorry that happened, Rony. No one should be treated that way. Did you tell the teacher or the principal?"

Rony: "No, I didn't. I was too scared. And I ran away."

Father asked with care.

"It's okay to be scared. It can happen to anybody, but you need to tell them when someone is hurting you. We can talk to the school and make sure it doesn't happen again. But you need to be brave and speak up."

Still, Rony was feeling sad and replied,

"But I don't want to go back there. They'll just bully me again."

His father tried to make him understand that this situation may occur at any stage of life.

"Rony, you can't let them win. You can't let bullies make you feel like you don't belong. You belong anywhere you want to be. And you have a right to an education. You cannot change the place and situation each time. You have to fight for yourself, for your rights. Accept this challenge and prove that you are not bullied by anyone. We'll talk to the school and make sure they understand what happened. But you can't give up. You're stronger than you think."

Rony felt reassured by his father's words but still felt scared and unsure about going back to school. He knew he needed to be brave, but it felt like a big challenge.

As soon as he entered the classroom the next day, he noticed that some of his classmates were giving him strange looks. During the break again these boys make fun of him.

He wanted to run away and hide, but he remembered his father's words. He knew that he couldn't let the bullies get the best of him.

After a few moments of silence, Rony stood up straight and looked into the eyes of the bullies.

He told them firmly but politely that he was not going to tolerate their behaviour and that he deserved to be treated with respect. He then walked away and joined a group of students who were playing outside.

Although Rony felt hurt and upset by the incident, he knew that he had done the right thing by standing up for himself. He also knew that he couldn't let the bullies get the best of him and that he had to keep his head up and stay strong.

Rony's teacher later discovered the incident and spoke to the students involved. She made it clear that bullying was unacceptable and that everyone in the class should treat each other with respect and kindness.

5

Adapting to the Village life

Rony found it difficult to adjust to the village school initially. He had grown up attending a prestigious school in the city, and the village school was very different. The classrooms were small, and the teaching methods were more traditional. The curriculum was also more focused on agriculture and rural life, which was a new and unfamiliar subject for Rony.

Rony struggled to make friends in the village school, as he was the only city boy in his class. The other students all seemed to know each other and were initially hesitant to include Rony in their activities. They were in doubt to approach him, and he felt isolated and alone. He also found it challenging to communicate with his classmates, as they spoke a different dialect than he was used to.

In addition to these challenges, Rony also found it difficult to keep up with his studies. The teaching methods in the village school were more rote-based, and Rony was used to a more conceptual and analytical approach to learning.

He found it hard to memorize the information he was given, and he felt like he wasn't learning anything new. Also, the school was much smaller and less well-equipped than the one he had attended in the city.

But still, Rony was firm enough to make the most of his time in the village school. He worked hard to learn the local dialect and to connect with his classmates.

He also sought help from his teachers to understand the subjects which he was struggling with.

As time goes by, Rony began to adjust to the environment. He found that he enjoyed learning about agriculture and rural life, and he was impressed by the knowledge and skills that the other children possessed. He also developed close friendships with some of his classmates and found that they were more accepting and welcoming than he had initially thought.

In the end, Rony overcame his initial struggles and learned valuable lessons about adapting to new environments and making the most of unfamiliar situations.

He came to appreciate the differences between city and village schools and realized that both had their unique strengths and weaknesses. Rony's positive attitude and willingness to embrace

New experiences helped him adjust to his new school and make new friends in the village.

6

The Road to Victory

Rony had been eagerly awaiting the district-level football matches for months. He had always loved playing football and had been practicing hard to form the school team. The football matches were started and after a series of matches, Rony's team made it to the final game. He had done very well till now for the school. And now his responsibility had increased. He was practicing hard for the finals.

The day of the final match arrived, and Rony was feeling a mix of excitement and nervousness. He knew that the competition would be tough, but he was resolved to give it his all.

As he stepped onto the field, Rony could feel the tension in the air. The opposing team was strong, and they had a large crowd of supporters cheering them on. But Rony was focused on the game and the task at hand and his parents were present to cheer him up.

The match began, and both teams played with intensity and skill. Rony's team was holding their own, but it was a close game. The score was tied for most of the match, and the tension was palpable. In the second half of the game, Rony got his chance to shine. He received the ball near the halfway line and dribbled past several defenders, weaving in and out with agility and speed. He made his way toward the goal and took a powerful shot.

The ball soared past the goalkeeper and hit the back of the net. The crowd erupted in cheers, and Rony's teammates lifted him in celebration.

Rony's goal gave his team a much-needed boost of confidence, and they continued to play with their willpower and heart. In the final minutes of the game, the opposing team made a valiant effort to equalize, but Rony and his teammates held strong. The final whistle blew, and Rony's team emerged as the victors. The players hugged each other in joy and relief, and Rony felt a sense of pride and accomplishment wash over him. He had played his best game yet, and he had helped his team win the championship. The victory was a testament to Rony's hard work and commitment to the sport. It also showed him that he could succeed and find acceptance in his new village home. He knew that he had found a new family in his teammates and that he had a place where he belonged.

After winning the final match of the district-level football tournament, Rony and his teammates were celebrated as heroes in the school. Students and teachers congratulated them and praised them for their impressive performance.

Rony felt a sense of pride and joy knowing that he had contributed to his team's success. He had made many new friends on the football team, and they had bonded over their shared love of the sport. The victory had brought them even closer together.

As Rony walked through the school hallways, he was greeted with high-fives and cheers from other students. Many of them looked up to him and admired him for his skills on the football field. Rony felt a sense of acceptance that he had never experienced before.

Rony's parents were proud of him, and his father was impressed by his son's accomplishments.

Rony's success on the football field had given him newfound confidence and a sense of purpose. He had found his passion in football, and he knew that he wanted to continue playing and improving. He had also learned the value of hard work, dedication, and teamwork, which he knew would serve him well in all aspects of his life.

In this way, the victory brought Rony and his team together and earned them the respect and admiration of their schoolmates. It was a moment that Rony would never forget, and it cemented his place in the village as a talented and accomplished football player.

Rony had become good friends with Rohit, Aarav, Dhruv, and Vansh. Their friendship formed over their shared love of football and their experiences of living in the village. Rony had proven himself on the football field, and his teammates respected and admired him.

The five boys formed a strong bond, as they spent more time together. They spent their afternoons playing football or exploring the village together. They had inside jokes and shared memories that brought them even closer together.

7

Friendship Forever

Rony was the natural leader of the group. He had a quiet confidence and a natural aura that drew the other boys to him. He was also the most experienced football player, and he often provided guidance and encouragement to his teammates.

Rohit was always the comedian of the group. He always had a smile on his face and loved to make his friends laugh with his jokes and gesture. Aarav was very particular about his thoughts and the thinker. He was always coming up with new strategies and ideas for their football games and explaining them in detail. Dhruv was the peacemaker. He had a calming presence and could diffuse any tension or conflicts that arose. Vansh was the newest member of the group, but he had quickly become a valuable teammate and friend.

Their friendship was built on mutual respect and support. They encouraged each other to be the best versions of themselves and to chase their dreams. They also had each other's backs, both on and off the football field.

As time passed, their friendship grew stronger. They faced challenges and hardships together, but they always emerged stronger and more resilient. They knew that they could rely on each other no matter what and that their bond would last a lifetime.

But it wasn't just football that brought them together.

They did everything together, from cycling around the village to walk to school every day. They were always sharing their lunch boxes, talking about their favourite TV shows, and playing together.

On weekends, they often visited each other's homes and play board games. They loved going on little adventures, like exploring nearby woods or discovering new bike trails. They even had a secret place where they would gather and make plans for their next adventure.

They had shared many experiences, both good and bad, and had learned to lean on each other for support.

Rony also learned a lot about himself during his time in the village. He had discovered strengths and talents he didn't know he had and as a result, he was improving day by day.

He was grateful for the experience of living in the village and knew that it had changed him in many ways. He had become humbler, more patient, and more empathetic toward others.

8

The Call of the Jungle

One day, while Rony was playing with his friend Rohit.

Rohit told him about the jungle that was near the village.

"Hey Rony, have you heard about the jungle near the village?"

Rony nodded.

"Yeah, I've heard about it. But I've never been there."

Rohit continued the conversation.

"You should come with me sometime. It's cool. But you have to be careful. There's a weird animal that people talk about."

Rony was pricking up.

"What kind of animal?"

Rohit placed his hand on Rony's shoulder and continued.

"I don't know. Some people say it's a big cat, like a leopard or something. Others say it's some kind of monster. But everyone agrees it's really scary."

Rony got a little serious and asked Rohit

"Are you serious? That sounds dangerous."

Rohit nodded in agreement.

"Yeah, it is. But we can go together and be careful. And if we see anything, we'll just run away."

Rony got very excited with the idea to explore something new. He decided to go with Rohit but promised himself he would be careful and watchful for anything dangerous.

The thought of a strange animal lurking near their village was a little unsettling, but the idea of exploring the jungle and possibly discovering something new was too tempting to resist.

Excited by their conversation about the jungle, Rony suggested to Rohit, "Why don't we plan a trip to the jungle together? We can explore it more and try to find that weird animal that people are talking about."

Rohit too was happy as Rony agreed to come with him.

The next day as Rony, Rohit, Aarav, Vansh, and Dhruv were playing outside,

Rony brought up the idea of exploring the jungle again.

"Hey guys, do you want to come to explore the jungle with me and Rohit? "

"Yeah, it'll be fun! We can see if we can find that weird animal people talk about." Rohit tried to make them understand.

Vansh looked hesitant.

"I don't know, Rony. That sounds dangerous. I don't want to get hurt."

Dhruv shook his head.

"Yeah, me too. I don't want to go if there's a monster or something in there."

"But guys, we'll be careful. We won't go too far in, and we'll stick together. It'll be an adventure!" Rony explained them.

Vansh and Dhruv still looked unsure, but Rony, Aarav, and Rohit were excited about the idea of exploring the jungle. They decided to wait and see if Vansh and Dhruv changed their minds, but Rony couldn't help feeling a little disappointed that his friends weren't as eager to explore as he was.

Vansh was still not ready.

"I'm not sure about this, guys. What if we run into a dangerous animal or get lost?"

Rony again persuaded Vansh.

"Don't worry, Vansh. We'll take precautions and stick together. We won't go too deep into the jungle either."

Rohit also agreed to Rony.

"Yeah, we'll make sure everything is safe. Plus, it'll be an adventure."

Aarav too joined Rony and Rohit with enthusiasm.

"Come on, Vansh. You can do it. It'll be fun."

Dhruva was also thought to be a part of these three boys. And explained to Vansh.

"And we'll be with you the whole time. We're all in this together."

Finally, Vansh is also ready with the plan.

"Okay, I guess I'll give it a try. But promise me that we'll be careful."

Rony: "We promise, Vansh."

Before going to the jungle, Rony and his friends planned carefully. They made a list of all the necessary equipment they needed, such as flashlights, a first aid kit, and food supplements. They also decided on a meeting point and time to start their journey, and when to return home.

Rony took the responsibility to gather all the required equipment and food supplements from his home without letting his parents know.

Rony was searching through his father's cupboard when he stumbled upon an old map of the village. He quickly grabbed it and took it to his friends. They all huddled around the map, excited to see what it contained.

9

Adventure on the way

Rony examined the map closely and showed his friends the different landmarks and areas of the village that they could explore. They were surprised to see that the jungle was marked on the map, and they could even see the different trails that led to it.

With the help of the map, they planned out their route and decided which trail to take to reach the jungle. They also marked out some key points on the map to ensure they didn't get lost on their journey.

Rony and his friends were thrilled to have found such a helpful tool, and they felt more confident and prepared for their adventure into the jungle. They carefully packed their bags and made

sure they had all the necessary equipment and supplements for the trip.

They also made a rough map of the area and marked some significant landmarks which they could easily find.

They discussed how to navigate through the jungle and decided to follow the river as it was an easy way to move forward. They also made sure to wear appropriate clothing and shoes for the jungle terrain.

As their parents were unaware of their plan, they planned to be back before nightfall.

Two days before the planned journey into the jungle, Dhruv started to feel more and more anxious. He was worried about the dangers that might be lurking in the jungle, and he didn't want to put himself in harm's way.

As the day of the trip grew closer, Dhruv's fear and anxiety became more and more intense. He talked to Rony and the others about his concerns, but they tried to reassure him that everything would be okay.

"Hey guys, Dhruv just called me and he's not going to be able to come with us to the jungle. He's too scared."

Rohit was quite angry.

"What? That's not fair. We've been planning this for weeks!"

Vansh raised Dhruv's concern.

"I don't blame him. The jungle sounds scary."

Aarav: "Come on, guys. We can't let Dhruv's fear stop us. We've got the map and we're all together. We can do this."

Rony talked in agreement,

"Aarav's right. We can't let one person's fear stop us from having an adventure. We'll just have to make sure we stick together and watch out for each other."

Rony's kind words and assurance made Dhruv ready to join in their adventure. Which gave immense pleasure to all of them.

Rony happily said,

"Hey Dhruv, we are really glad that you decided to come with us. We know it's not easy for you, but we promise to look out for each other and have a great time.

Rohit also replied with happiness, "Yeah, we're a team, remember? We stick together no matter what.

Aarav: And we'll make sure you feel comfortable every step of the way. We wouldn't leave anyone behind.

Vansh: You don't have to worry about anything, Dhruv. We'll have fun and come back before you know it.

Rony repeated the plan, "We will go there at our school time and will return home as usual when we come from school. So, are you ready to do this?

Dhruv: Yeah, I am. Thanks for being such great friends, guys.

The day of exploring the jungle has arrived. Rony, Rohit, Aarav, Vansh, and Dhruv woke up early and got ready for their adventure. Rony had packed some snacks, water bottles, and a first aid kit in his backpack. He decided to take all his gadgets with him while exploring the jungle. He packed his backpack with his smartwatch, camera, binoculars, drone, and flashlight.

Rohit was amazed by seeing so many gadgets with Rony.

"Whoa, Rony. You're bringing all that stuff with you?"

Rony smiled and said, "Yeah, why not? We might see something cool in there and I want to capture it on camera."

Vansh also doubted the gadgets and gave his opinion on this.

"But what if we run into that scary animal people talk about? Will your gadgets help us?"

Rony was pretty sure: "Well, my smartwatch has GPS and I can use it to call for help if we need it. And the flashlight can help us see if it gets dark."

Dhruv was also not sure to keep gadgets with them.

"I don't know, Rony. It just seems like a lot of stuff to carry around."

But Rony undoubtedly said, "It's okay, guys. I'm used to carrying this stuff around. And who knows, we might need it for something else too."

Rohit: "Yeah, like if we see some cool birds or something. We can use the binoculars to get a closer look."

Vansh and Dhruv still looked a little skeptical, but Rony was determined to be prepared for anything they might encounter in the jungle. He slung his backpack over his shoulder and led the way into the dense forest.

As they left their houses and walked towards the village outskirts, the sun was just beginning to rise. It was around 6 AM. The air was cool and crisp, and the birds were chirping in the trees. The boys chatted and joked as they walked, feeling the thrill of anticipation building up inside them. When they reached the edge of the village, they stopped to check the map and make sure they were going in the right direction. Rony led the way, holding the map in his hand, while Rohit followed closely behind, carrying a compass. Aarav and Vansh walked on either side of them, and Dhruv brought up the rear.

As Rony, Rohit, Vansh, Aarav, and Dhruv entered the jungle for the first time, they were filled with a mix of excitement and trepidation. The dense foliage and the sound of rustling leaves and chirping birds made them feel like they were in a completely different world.

10

Lost in the wilderness

Rony was experiencing this environment for the very first time.

"Wow, this is so cool! I feel like we're in a movie or something."

Rohit: "Yeah, and the air feels so fresh and clean. I love it!"

Vansh's fear was still in his mind.

"It's a little scary though, don't you think? I keep thinking I'll see that weird animal people talk about."

Dhruv was also scared.

"Me too. And what if we get lost here? It all looks the same."

Rony reassured them frequently.

"Don't worry, guys. We'll stick together and we won't go too far in."

Rohit observed and said, "And look, there's a little stream over there. Maybe we can follow it and see where it leads."

As they walked further into the jungle, they felt more and more like explorers on an adventure. The sights and sounds of the forest were all around them, and they couldn't wait to see what they would discover next.

As they walked deeper into the jungle, they could hear the sounds of rustling leaves and twigs snapping under their feet. The boys felt a sense of adventure as they explored the unknown terrain, with no one else around for miles.

As they five were walking for almost 3-4 hours, all of them now felt hungry. It was around noon. Rony, Rohit, and Dhruv were exhausted and hungry. They found a big mango tree and decided to take a break and have their lunch which they had brought with them from home.

Rony got tired. "I can't go any further without food. Let's take a break here and have lunch."

Rohit: "Good idea. We need to keep up our energy if we're going to find that animal."

Dhruv: "I'm so hungry, I can eat anything."

They all sat down under the shade of the mango tree and started to eat their lunch. They shared their food and talked about their experiences in the jungle so far.

Rony: "This is amazing. I never knew we could find such a beautiful spot in the jungle."

Rohit: "Yeah, it's nice to take a break and enjoy the scenery."

After finishing their lunch and taking some rest, they felt recharged and ready to continue their search for the animal. They packed up their things and started walking deeper into the jungle, with a renewed sense of determination to find the weird animal.

As Rony, Rohit, Vansh, Aarav, and Dhruv walked deeper into the jungle,

they came across a very narrow trail. To pass through it, they had to walk in a line, one after the other where Rony led the line and Dhruv was the last member. As they were walking, suddenly, they heard a strange sound of something falling, and Vansh disappeared from their sight.

Rony shouted.

"Vansh! Where did you go?"

Rohit also worried.

"Vansh! Answer us!"

Dhruv: "Oh no, this isn't good. What if he's hurt?"

Rony took the lead and replied.

"We have to find him. Come on!"

They started to look for Vansh, calling out his name and listening for any response. But there was no answer, only the sound of rustling leaves and the occasional chirp of a bird. They walked further into the jungle, trying to retrace their steps and find any sign of their missing friend.

Rohit moved everyone's attention to one place.

"Hey guys, look over there. Is that his shoe?"

Dhruv said nervously, "Oh no, it is! Something must have happened to him."

However, Rony was undaunted and encouraged them.

"We have to keep looking. And be careful, who knows what could be out here."

With a sense of urgency and fear, they continued their search, hoping to find Vansh safe and sound.

11

Search For Missing Friend

Rohit, Aarav, and Dhruv were scared and didn't know what to do. Rony, who had a bit more composure, suggested that they should split up and search for Vansh. Rohit and Aarav agreed, but Dhruv was hesitant and wanted to go back.

Rony convinced Dhruv that they couldn't leave Vansh alone and that they needed to find him. They split up and searched the area for Vansh, calling out his name at regular intervals.

As they searched, they started to get worried and scared. They had no idea where they were or what was going to happen. They continued to call out Vansh's name, but there was still no response. They decided to meet back at the mango tree after an hour, and if they still couldn't find Vansh, they would go back and inform their parents.

As they were searching, suddenly they heard a loud and scary sound coming from Dhruv's direction. They quickly ran towards the sound, calling Dhruv's name, but there was no response.

Rony started calling Dhruv loudly.

"Dhruv! Dhruv! Where are you?"

Rohit said worriedly. "This is getting scary. What if something has happened to him?"

Aarav: "We need to find him. Let's split up and search this area."

They searched for Dhruv for several minutes, but he was nowhere to be found. They were getting worried and scared.

Now even Rony was scared and said in a worried tone. "This is not good. We need to find him quickly."

Rohit: "Let's keep looking. He couldn't have gone too far."

Aarav guessed, "Maybe he's stuck somewhere. We should check around the trees and bushes."

They continued searching for Dhruv, calling his name and looking around the trees and bushes, but there was no sign of him. They started to get more and more worried and wondered what could have happened to him.

As the night began to fall, the group of boys felt a sense of fear creeping up on them. They were lost in the dense jungle and two of their friends were missing. They searched for Vansh and Dhruv frantically but they were nowhere to be found.

As the night fell, Rony, Rohit, and Aarav started to feel more scared and helpless. They had been searching for Vansh and Dhruv for hours, but still couldn't find them.

Rony broke the silence, "What are we going to do now? It's getting dark, and we still haven't found them."

Rohit also didn't know what to do, "I don't know. We can't keep searching in the dark. It's too dangerous."

Aarav also expressed his thoughts, "I think a weird animal caught Vansh and Dhruv. we should go back and inform our parents. They can help us search for them tomorrow."

But Rony was not ready to go back to the village, "But what if something has happened to them? We can't just leave them here."

Rohit started to explain to Rony, "We don't have a choice, Rony. We need to go back and get help."

Reluctantly, they started to make their way back to the mango tree. As they walked, they kept calling out for Vansh and Dhruv, hoping to hear a response.

But the jungle was quiet and eerie in the darkness, and there was no sign of their friends. They finally reached the mango tree, feeling defeated and panicked.

Rony: "We couldn't find them. What are we going to do now?"

Rohit was firm in his opinion, "Let's go back and tell our parents. They will know what to do."

Aarav: "We can't just leave them here. What if they're hurt or lost?"

Now Rony clearly understood the situation and decided to inform his parents first,

"I know, but we can't search in the dark. It's too dangerous. We need to go back and get help."

They finally decided to go back and inform their parents about what had happened. They knew it was the right thing to do, but they still felt scared and helpless, hoping that their friends would be found safe and sound. Unfortunately, at this point, Rony looked at his smartwatch and tried to use the GPS to navigate their way back to the village. However, there was no network signal in the dense jungle. They were completely lost and terrified. They huddled together, hoping for someone to come and rescue them.

12

Stranded in the jungle at night

The night was getting darker, and the boys were feeling hungry and thirsty. They had never felt so helpless and alone before. It was around 8 PM. Rony, Rohit, and Aarav decided to camp for the night in the jungle as it was too dark to search for Vansh anymore.

They were afraid and anxious. Rony tried to keep everyone calm and composed. He suggested they light a bonfire and take turns keeping watch for any sign of Vansh. They all huddled together around the bonfire, trying to stay warm and hoping for Vansh's safe return.

Here in the village, parents were tense as their kids were not coming home from school for a long time. Rony's parents thought the children must have been playing together after school so, Rony did not come home till now.

But when it was too late, they got worried. They rushed to school but after visiting the school they came to know that the five were not coming to the school today. and they were shocked.

The parents of the missing children immediately started searching for them in the nearby areas. They informed the local authorities and sought their help. The news spread like wildfire in the village, and everyone started looking for the children. The parents were extremely worried and feared the worst. They couldn't imagine what could have happened to their innocent children. They prayed for their safe return. The entire village was on high alert and ready to do anything to find the missing children.

Police decided to search with the parents. When Rony's father was getting ready to go out for a search, he opened the cupboard and realized that his map

was missing. Now he understood that children might be in the jungle because only the forest part of the entire village remained to be explored by them.

Rony's father immediately informed the police and the other parents that the children might be in the jungle. He showed them another map and explained how the children loved to explore the jungle. The police, with the help of the parents, decided to search the jungle. They were equipped with flashlights and other necessary equipment. It was around 2 AM.

Rohit and Aarav blamed themselves for letting Vansh go alone and were inconsolable with fear. Rony tried to comfort them and assured them that they would find Vansh and Dhruv in the morning. Both the kids and their parents were scared and worried, not knowing what would happen next.

As the night wore on, they could hear strange noises in the jungle which made

them even more scared. Rony knew he had to keep his friends safe, and he kept them occupied by talking about their past experiences together and cracking jokes. However, the fear of Vansh's disappearance loomed over their heads.

Despite the fear and uncertainty, they all tried to get some sleep, hoping for a better tomorrow where they would find their friend.

Rony's mind was racing with thoughts of the day that had just passed. He remembered waking up in the morning with a sense of excitement for their jungle adventure. The wind was blowing gently, and the sun was about to rise, as they set out on their journey. The chirping of birds and the rustling of leaves added to the beauty of the moment. But now, as he stood there in the dense jungle, his eyes wandered around his surroundings. The once beautiful and peaceful place now seemed like a scary and dangerous jungle. He could feel the sweat trickling down his forehead, and his heart beating fast.

Rony couldn't believe how quickly things had turned bad. They had lost two of their friends, and they were now stranded in the jungle with no food or water. His thoughts were interrupted by a sudden noise, and he quickly turned around, hoping to see Dhruv or Vansh. But there was no one. Rony could feel the fear creeping in as he realized that they were all alone in the jungle, with no way out.

Rony's heart raced as he stared at the footprints. He examined the footprints carefully and noticed that they were not of the weird animal that they had heard about earlier. The footprints were human, but they were much larger than any of their own. They were unmistakably human, and they led towards a dense jungle in the distance. He immediately alerted his friends, and they all gathered around the footprints in awe.

He thought to himself, "Who could it be in the jungle at this hour?"

He wondered if it was the same person or people who were responsible for Vansh and Dhruv's disappearance. Rony's mind was racing with all kinds of thoughts, and he couldn't stop it. He was worried about the safety of his friends and himself.

"What could it be?" Rohit wondered aloud.

"Maybe it's the creature people have been talking about," Aarav said, half-jokingly.

Rony's mind raced with possibilities. Were these the footprints of someone who could help them find their lost friends? Or were they made by someone or something that could cause them harm? As Rony examined the footprints closely with his hi-tech binoculars, he noticed that they were quite large and seemed to have been made by someone wearing boots recently. He could see that the footprints were heading in a particular direction, and they seemed to lead deeper into the jungle.

Rony's curiosity got the better of him, and he decided to follow the footprints.

13

The Kidnapping Conspiracy

He pulled up a map on his smartwatch and compared it to the footprints, trying to determine where they might lead. Rony couldn't help but feel a sense of unease wash over him as he realized they were likely dealing with someone or something much bigger and potentially dangerous than they had anticipated.

"Guys, these footprints are human, but they're way too big to be Vansh's or Dhruv's. We need to be careful," Rony warned the group. Rohit and Aarav nodded in agreement, but their faces were etched with worry. They all knew that they were in uncharted territory, and the prospect of encountering something dangerous was becoming more and more real. Despite their fear, they decided to follow the footprints, hoping that they would lead them to some kind of safety or help.

Rony, the gadget enthusiast, decided to use his drone to help locate his friends. He quickly set up his drone and launched it into the air, using the live feed from the drone's camera to search for any signs of Dhruv's location.

As he was searching, Rony noticed something unusual in the distance. It was a glimmer of light that seemed to be coming from a small hut nearby. He directed the drone towards the hut and saw a figure lying on the ground inside. It was Dhruv! Rony flew his drone closer to the window of the hut and saw that Dhruv's hands were tied behind his back, and his mouth was covered with duct tape.

He quickly realized that his friend was in danger and needed to be rescued immediately.

Rony landed his drone outside the hut. They carefully followed the tracks, making sure to stay alert for any signs of

danger. Rony peeked in through the window first but no one appeared inside. Slowly they moved forward. As the group entered the hut, they found that no one was there other than Dhruv.

Dhruv, who was very scared, got happy when he saw Rony coming. Rony quickly removed the duct tape from his mouth and helped him to his feet. Dhruv was so happy that he hugged Rony and started talking loudly in excitement. But Rony mentioned him being quiet. They carefully followed the tracks, making sure to stay alert for any signs of danger. However, they did not lose hope and decided to search the place thoroughly for any clue. After all, they had to find Vansh as well. After a few minutes of searching, they found an old parchment lying on the floor. It seemed to be a map of some kind with strange markings on it. Rony examined the map closely.

Rohit looked at the map and said with excitement,

"Friends! This map is same as shown in the movies." Aarav was also amused to see it. He added,

"Guys, we will get some clues from this map."

Dhruv said with a feeling of having gained something," Maybe we will find something out of it related to Vansh."

Rony thought for a while and realized that it was a treasure map. He immediately shared this information with Rohit and Aarav, who were equally excited. They had heard of such legends before but had never thought they would stumble upon a treasure map themselves.

As they studied the map, they noticed that it was pointing toward a nearby cave. It was clear that this was the only lead they had in finding their missing friend. They knew they had to investigate the cave and see if there was any connection to the footprints they had found earlier. Rony, Rohit, and Aarav were thrilled to see Dhruv alive and well. However, they were also very curious about where he had been the previous day. After coming outside of the hut, the three friends approached Dhruv and started questioning him.

Rony: "Hey, Dhruv! Thank God, you're safe. Where have you been? We were so worried about you."

Dhruv remained silent, looking with fear in his eyes.

Rohit: "Come on, boy. You can tell us now. We won't get mad at you or anything and will not stop you. We just want to know where you've been all this time."

Aarav: "Yeah, we were so scared for you. Please tell us what happened."

Dhruv finally spoke up. He was telling the other three boys that while he was searching for Vansh alone in one direction, suddenly a strange man, who covered his whole face, came closer to me and closed my mouth. And took me here."

Rony and the other boys were shocked to hear this. They asked Dhruv if he could recognize the man or remember anything else, but Dhruv said he couldn't as he didn't see his face. Rony suggested that they should try to retrace their steps and look for any clues that could lead them to Vansh and the mysterious man.

14

The Great Escape

Now the important task was to look for Vansh in the cave.

Rony knew that if he wanted to find Vansh in the cave, they had to come prepared as the mysterious man might be in the cave.

Rony, Rohit, Aarav, and Dhruv sat together to make a plan to explore the cave where they suspected the stranger might be. They decided to take precautions and prepare themselves in case of any danger. They first decided to carry torches, a first-aid kit, and some cudgels.

They also agreed to move slowly and quietly, avoiding making any noise that might alert the stranger.

Rony suggested that they should have a secret code or signal to communicate with each other in case they get separated.

Aarav shouted, "Ka-Ka-Ka-Ka-kow-kow..."

All were laughing.

"Ok, we all can make the sound of the cuckoo bird, right? just like Aarav. If we got separated in the middle or felt any danger, we used to make this sound."

They all agreed to it and decided on that specific signal. They also agreed to stay close to each other and move into a group.

They then discussed the possible locations where their friend and the treasure might be hidden in the cave. They decided to first search for their friend, and then continue the search for the treasure.

Finally, they all agreed on the plan and set out to explore the cave, ready for any obstacles or danger that may come their way.

As the boys reached the entrance of the cave, Rony quickly sent his drone inside to scout the area and check for any potential danger. He connected the drone's live feed to his smartwatch so he could monitor the surroundings while keeping a safe distance from the cave.

While the drone was scanning the area, Rony used his binoculars to look closer at the cave entrance and the surroundings. He noticed that several men were guarding the entrance with weapons.

Rony quickly informed the others and came up with a plan. He sent his drone to fly above the cave and distract the guards, while the other boys made their way inside using the map to navigate.

He also used the watch to scan for any heat signatures or potential threats. It was 4 AM and the sun would shine in just 2 more hours.

As they got closer to the spot marked on the treasure map, they heard Vansh's voice coming from a nearby place. Rony quickly sent his drone to investigate the place and gather information.

Using the drone's camera, Rony was able to locate Vansh and the men who had kidnapped him. Rony quickly activated the emergency signal on his smartwatch by climbing on a tall tree, which alerted the police and called for backup.

While waiting for help to arrive, Rony used his drone to distract and disorient the kidnappers, while the other boys freed Vansh and made their way out of the cave. With the help of his gadgets and quick thinking, Rony was able to save Vansh and bring him back to safety. But kidnappers came to know about Rony and his friends.

As the kidnappers were following them, Rony quickly gathered his friends and told them to run with him. Meanwhile, he also used his drone to distract the kidnappers by flying it around and making loud noises.

Rony also used his binoculars to spot any potential danger ahead and guide his friends through the dense forest.

As they were running, the kidnappers were getting closer, but Rony had a plan. He instructed his friends to hide in a nearby bush while he used his flashlight to blind the kidnappers and confuse them with the loud sounds of his Bluetooth speaker.

Finally, the police arrived and took control of the situation. Rony and his friends were safe, and Vansh was rescued from the kidnappers' hideout in the cave. The boys were praised for their bravery and resourcefulness, and Rony's use of his gadgets helped to save their lives.

15

Heroes Among Us

After the police arrested the kidnappers, they were interrogated to know about the rumors about the weird animal in the jungle. The kidnappers confessed that they spread the rumor of the animal to keep people away from the jungle, as they didn't want anyone to find out about their treasure. They knew that people would be afraid to enter the jungle because of the rumour about the animal and it would help them to hide their treasure. The kidnappers also revealed that they created strange sounds to scare people away from the jungle.

The police searched the jungle and found the treasure hidden inside a cave, which was guarded by the kidnappers. The treasure included gold coins, jewels, and valuable artifacts. The parents of all the boys were relieved to see their children safe and sound.

After the incident, the police advised people to not believe in rumors and to always inform the authorities if they find any suspicious activity or if someone goes missing.

Rony and his friend's parents were extremely proud of their children's bravery and quick thinking in the face of danger.

They were relieved that their children had returned home safely and praised them for their courage and determination.

Rony's father was especially proud of him for using his gadgets to fight against the kidnappers and help his friends. He realized that his son's love for technology could be used for good and encouraged him to continue to explore and learn more about it.

The parents of all the boys also learned a valuable lesson about the importance of trust and communication with their children. They realized that it was important to give their children the freedom to explore and grow, but also to make sure that they were always aware of their surroundings and had a way to reach them in case of emergency.

Overall, the parents were grateful to have such brave and smart children and were happy to support them in their future adventures and endeavors.

After some days of a gap, Rony again asked casually with a laugh to Rohit.

Rony: "Hey Rohit, should we plan another adventure trip soon?"

Rohit: "Ha-ha, are you serious Rony? After all these things happened to us, you still want to go on another trip?"

Rony understood Rohit's concern and replied

"Come on, Rohit! You know one bad experience cannot stop us from having fun and exploring new places. also, this time we'll be more careful and take all necessary precautions."

Aarav: "I agree with Rony. It was a scary experience, but it also showed us how strong we can be when we work together. Let's plan another trip soon!"

Dhruv: "Count me in too! But this time, I'm not leaving anyone's side."

Rohit: "Okay fine, I guess I'm in too. But let's make sure to inform our parents and take all safety measures before we go."

www.ingramcontent.com/pod-product-compliance
Lightning Source LLC
LaVergne TN
LVHW021201160826
845679LV00024B/2203

* 9 7 9 8 8 9 3 6 3 6 0 8 6 *